nickelodeon

SpongeBob SquarePants

Bunny Business

Illustrated by Dave Aikins

A GOLDEN BOOK • NEW YORK

created by

Stephen Hillenburg

ISBN: 978-0-375-86818-4
www.randomhouse.com/kids
MANUFACTURED IN CHINA
10 9 8 7 6 5 4 3 2

"Ahh . . . spring is here!"

"It's time to get back to nature."

"I'm a flower child."

Patrick is getting his garden ready.
Will you draw some flowers for him?

Time for a spring cleaning!

Find the path that will help SpongeBob put away his winter things.

START

FINISH

ANSWER:

"When cleaning, don't forget to floss."

"Now comes the most special
part of spring—Easter!"

"I love holidays!"

"I'm feeling eggy!"

"You can't have Easter without eggs!"

"One order of eggs coming right up, SpongeBob!"

"Each egg will be a work of art."

"Sometimes you have to color outside the lines."

"I'm an egg-cellent artist!"

"This is one good-looking egg."

"This egg will be the *star* of the basket!"

"I'm making a mess."

"Let's get these eggs into some Easter baskets."

Circle the Patrick who is different.

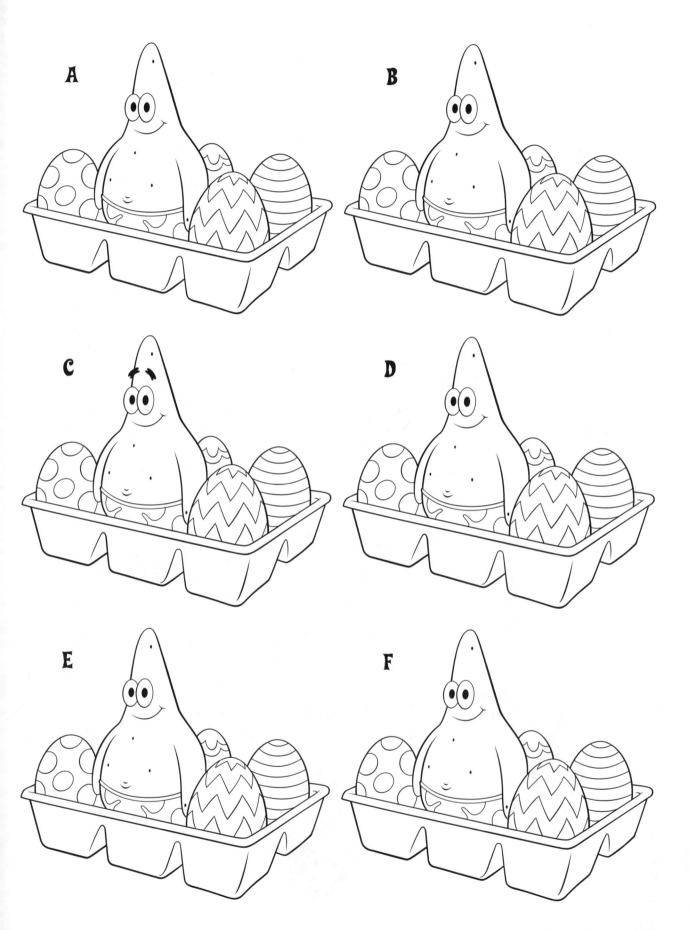

A

B

C

D

E

F

ANSWER: C.

Ready for delivery!

"Now let's deliver these eggs
to everyone in Bikini Bottom."

"We need costumes to deliver these eggs!"

"These costumes will be perfect."

"Let's go to work."

"First stop: Squidward's house."

"Burglar!"

"Maybe these weren't the right costumes, Patrick."

"Let's be bunnies!"

"I've always wanted a fluffy tail!"

Draw some bunny ears on Patrick.

Follow the key to color Patrick's bunny costume.

1 = Pink   2 = Blue   3 = Brown
4 = Green   5 = Yellow

"Let's do some bunny business!"

"Let's deliver eggs to the Krusty Krab. Help us find the way."

START

THE KRUSTY KRAB

FINISH

ANSWER:

"Would you like an egg with your Krabby Patty?"

"I have a gift that you'll really like!"

"Is it money? I really like money!"

"Happy Easter, Mr. Krabs!"

"Here's an Easter egg for you, Plankton."

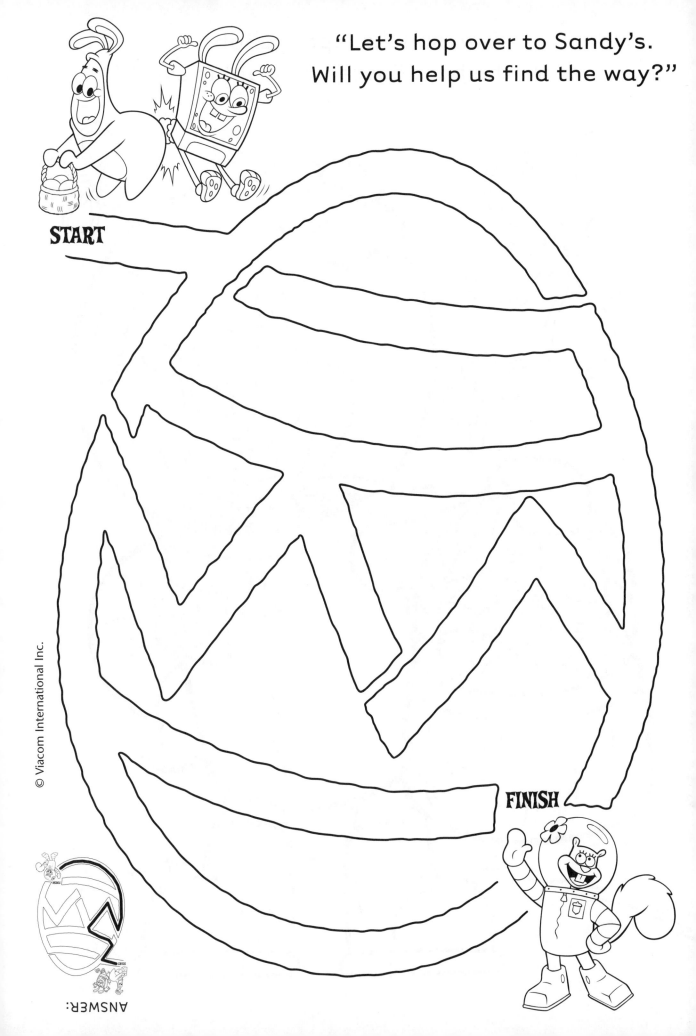

"Let's hop over to Sandy's.
Will you help us find the way?"

START

FINISH

© Viacom International Inc.

ANSWER:

"Aw, shucks, SpongeBob!
You're the best Easter jackrabbit ever!"

"Hoppy Easter, Sandy!"

"Since you two are my favorite Easter critters, I've got gifts for you."

"You can't have Easter
without chocolate bunnies."

How many jelly beans are there?

Will you draw a nutty Easter bonnet for Sandy?

SpongeBob needs a fancy Easter hat.

Squidward is dressed in his Easter best!

It's the Bikini Bottom Easter Parade!

"We can play games with our Easter eggs!"

"Let's have an Easter egg hunt!"

© Viacom International Inc.

Eggs can be hidden in the silliest places.

What an egg-cellent day!

Can you match each egg at the left to its character's shadow?

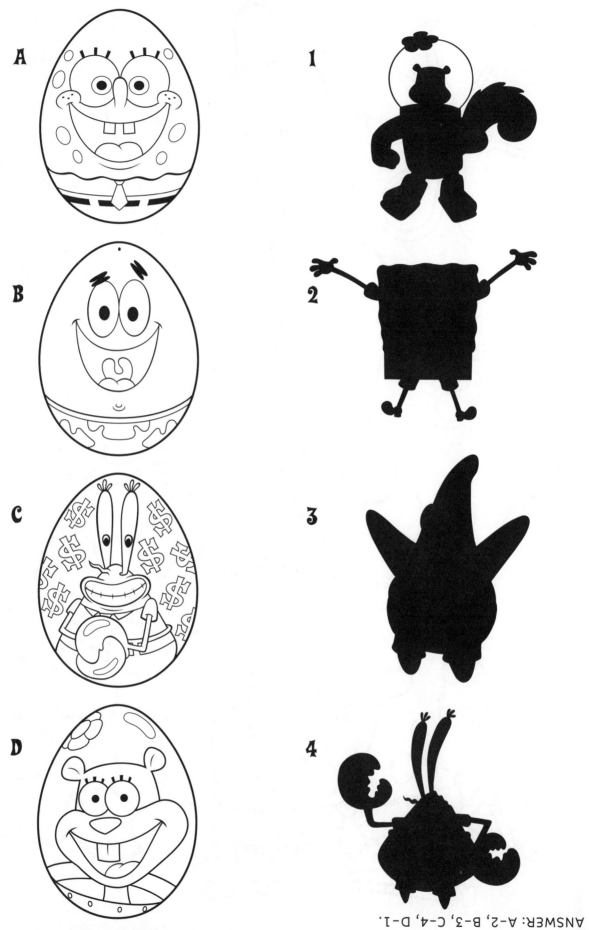

A

B

C

D

1

2

3

4

"I love finding eggs!"

"These eggs lead to my house. I wonder who delivered them. . . ."

"Gary! You're my Easter . . . *snail!*"

"Gary, you've made this the best Easter ever!"

Will you give Gary's shell some Easter decorations?

"Happy Easter, everyone!"